MW01097679

# Storm in Stone County

Book 7

The Cowboy Ranch Series

written by:

Kim Anderson Stone

Cover Photo: Kim Stone

Edited by: Lindsay Boone

**The events depicted in this book are purely fictitious. Any similarity to any person or persons is merely coincidental.**

This book is dedicated to all of the children who lost so much during Hurricane Michael.

The way these young people have held it together when the adults have fallen apart is such an inspiration to our whole community.

October 10, 2018 was not our darkest hour, but our brightest hours, as we stood together... united.

# Storm in Stone County

## The Cowboy Ranch Series

Chapter One

It had been a hot summer in Stone County. Matter of fact, Cody Cowboy couldn't remember it ever being this hot on the Cowboy Ranch. Cody, the oldest of the two Cowboy brothers, stopped by the barn one more time to check on his younger brother, Clint. Cody, who was 13 and very responsible for his age, knew he better keep an eye on 7 year old Clint.

Clint was mischievous and never missed an opportunity to get into trouble. When Cody found his little brother, he was surprised to see him actually finishing up his chores. "Cody, I'm glad to see you. Would you come help me get this bucket down? Ol' Boloney has got it stuck something fierce," said Clint.

Cody smiled as he walked to the end of the barn to Boloney's stall. Boloney was the oldest pony on the ranch, but he had never learned to behave. Boloney was usually out roaming the ranch or in Mama Cowboy's garden instead of being where he was supposed to be.

Ol' Boloney and young Clint were a lot alike, Cody reckoned. Both of them were always in some sort of mischief. This time, Boloney had flipped his water bucket over and somehow gotten it stuck in the feed pan.

Together, the boys pushed and pulled and finally got the water bucket back where it belonged.

"Cody, how you reckon ol' Boloney did that?  I was trying to be good to him and get him fresh water because it's hot as blue blazes.   Reckon what 'blue blazes' is anyway?   That's what Grandpa always says, 'hot as blue blazes.'  I don't know, but it's sure hot. Did you hear it thundering awhile ago? I did.  I hope we get some rain.  We need rain, don't we, Cody?   I ain't never seen it so hot,"  Clint said all in one breath.

Cody was used to his brother talking like this. Clint was wide open in everything he did. Cody looked over at his brother, punched him playfully on the shoulder and said, "Don't let Mama hear you say 'ain't,' Clint. She'll have you washing dishes for a week!"

Clint punched him back and said, "You don't be telling, ok? Washing dishes is for girls, ain't it; I mean, isn't it?" Both boys busted out laughing.

The boys went back to their chores, finishing up just as Daddy Cowboy pulled up on the tractor. They stood there in the doorway of the barn, looking just alike, except for the size of them. All three of the Cowboy guys were hot and sweaty. They may have been kind of stinky, too.

Mama Cowboy came out of the kitchen door and onto the porch. She was about to call them to come eat, but she changed her mind after seeing how dirty they were.

Mama Cowboy said, "Why don't we take the dogs down to the lake and let them swim awhile. It wouldn't hurt for you to jump in yourselves." Quick as a flash, Cody and Clint took off towards the lake.

Otis, the big white English bulldog, ran after them. Gibbs, the old fat beagle, waddled along with Daddy and Mama Cowboy. He threw his head back and let out a booo-roooo howl, pretending to hunt like he did when he was young.

Down by the lake, Otis waded out to his neck, seeming to enjoy the cool water.

The boys skinned off their clothes down to their underwear and were soon swimming like fish.

Old Gibbs waddled out into the water. Gibbs loved to swim. In his younger days, he could swim across the creek when he was tracking a deer. Now he just made little laps, being careful to turn around and come back to the edge before going out too deep.

Mama Cowboy looked over at Daddy Cowboy and said, "In you go, too, old man. It's a good thing we live out here all by ourselves because you're needing to skin out to your underwear, too!" Before long, the Cowboy men were all three in the lake. Yes sir. Living on the ranch was the best life ever.

Chapter Two

That evening, the family sat at the dinner table a little bit longer than usual making plans for the next day. Clint asked, "Mama, are we going in to town tomorrow for the Farmer's Market? I want to see my friends. I'll help you, though. I don't smell pies baking. Why don't I smell pies? You always take pies to sell at the market. You ok, Mama?"

Mama Cowboy looked over at her husband and busted out laughing.

"Clint, we aren't going to the market tomorrow. We have new neighbors who just moved in to that old ranch house by the creek. They are the Smiths. They have two children about your age, too. I think the girl's name is Fallon, and the boy is River."

Clint brightened up. "I'll go meet that boy, but you can meet the girl, Cody. You like girls, don't you, Cody?" Clint giggled as he made faces at his brother.

Mama said, "Everybody from town is meeting out at the Smiths' place to welcome them and help them get settled. I think Henry and Jessie Brooke Welder, along with Hank, will be there to help. I know Kate and Sarah Rose Tucker will be there, too."

At the mention of Sarah Rose, young Clint's cheeks turned bright pink. It was Cody's turn to do a little teasing. Clint thought Sarah Rose was the prettiest little girl in Stone County. He followed her like a new calf any time she was around.

Sarah Rose was as sweet as she was pretty and always willing to help someone else when they needed it.

Later on, long after the boys were in bed and the dogs were snoring on the porch swing, Daddy and Mama Cowboy sat on the porch like they did every evening. Off in the distance, lightning danced across the sky. Daddy said, "I sure wish that lightning would bring some rain. I'm worried about our crops this year. It's so dry. I can't remember it ever being so hot and dry this time of year, even with it being summer."

"I'm just praying we get some relief soon. I'd love to smell rain coming, but all I smell lately is dust and sweaty cowboys," Mama Cowboy teased.

With that, they stood and went inside, bringing an end to another day.

Chapter Three

Morning dawned bright and hot. The Cowboy family made quick work of their chores. Clint took extra time to make sure every water bucket was filled with fresh water and tied down so it couldn't be dumped over. It was going to be another hot day for sure.

He filled two buckets for Otis and Gibbs and tied them to the barn post. He wanted to make sure they didn't get knocked over. He knew that, as hot as it was, all the farm animals needed lots of water.

At the last minute, he set a smaller pan down and filled it with water. Lately, Cody had been seeing an old yellow cat sneaking around the barn, hunting for rats. He reckoned that if the cat was hunting, then he needed fresh water, too.

The boys had started trying to get the old cat to come to them, but so far, he kept his distance. They had started calling him "Scout" because that's what he did all day: scout for rats and mice. Clint came in the barn and saw what Cody was doing.

"It's a good thing Otis and Gibbs don't mind a cat being around. That Scout looks like he could whoop both of them," Clint declared. Cody had to agree. That was one rangy looking tom cat.

Before long, the Cowboy family had loaded up the truck with the supplies they thought they may need and were about to leave. Daddy Cowboy gave the command, "Stay" to Otis and Gibbs, and both dogs took their place on the porch to watch the ranch.

As the truck headed down the long driveway, Daddy Cowboy looked in the mirror and saw Otis still sitting at attention. He laughed out loud when he saw that Gibbs was already fast asleep in the swing. Some guard dog he was.

Looking back to the west, Daddy Cowboy noticed some dark clouds beginning to form. As they drove to the Smiths' place, Daddy Cowboy asked, "You see those clouds, boys? I sure hope it brings us some rain, don't you?"

"I do, too, Daddy. But, that cloud looks kind of scary. It's dark and looks like a line is drawn across the sky. Kind of like it's fine here, but way off over there, a big storm is brewing," said Cody.

Mama Cowboy said, "Well, as much as we need that rain, I hope it holds off until this evening. We need to get our new neighbors settled in."

The whole family was looking forward to meeting their new neighbors.

The one thing about Stone County that could be counted on was that everybody pitched in when somebody needed help.

Chapter Four

Billy and Maggie Smith, along with their children, River and Fallon, had chosen to move to Stone County from down near the beach after a terrible hurricane tore their house all to pieces awhile back. After trying for months to get their house fixed, they just decided that maybe a fresh start would be best.

Their cousin, Dylan West, would be living with them for a while because he had lost his home, too. Dylan brought his dog, Layla, with him. As a border collie, Layla could help out on the new ranch when they got cows.

The three young people still talked about the night that the storm hit. They'd never seen anything like the wind and rain. Dylan said his mom covered him in blankets in the hallway, and he felt like he would smother because it was so hot; all around them, trees snapped and windows crashed.

When the storm was over and they were able to go outside, they just couldn't believe what they saw. Everything was just ... broken. Fallon had run to the barn to check on her horses. Maggie had found her there, crying and holding her oldest horse.

Every animal seemed to be ok. Maggie remembered holding her young daughter and being very thankful that they all were alive and unharmed. They had lived through the worst storm ever to hit the beach. If they could live through that, then they would be strong enough to do anything, as long as they were together.

After finding a place in Stone County and making up their minds to move, River, Fallon, and Dylan were very anxious about starting school in the fall.

Everything that they knew as normal was taken from them by that ugly storm. Maybe meeting some of their new classmates before school started would help. They'd know soon enough because it looked like the whole county was beginning to pull up at their farmhouse.

Soon, the new neighbors were welcoming what seemed like the whole county! The men went right to work, mending fences and repairing the horse stalls. The women sat on the porch to get to know each other.

Before long, they had put together a plan on how best to help Maggie get her house unpacked and in order.

Maggie's mother, Mrs. Patsy, had made the trip with them. It didn't lake long to figure out that Mrs. Patsy was full of mischief herself. More than once that day, Mrs. Patsy would sneak away and be playing with the children in the yard instead of unpacking.

She even caught a lizard and gave it to Clint. It didn't take Clint long to be chasing the girls around the yard and making them squeal with laughter.

Mrs. Patsy, it seemed, was just a little bit of an instigator when it came to laughter and jokes. It looked as though the whole Smith family would fit right in Stone County like they had always been there.

Around lunch time, a school bus pulled into the yard. The doors opened, and kids came tumbling out.

Cody looked up and exclaimed, "Oh my gosh!!! Mr. Watts is here! And there's Mrs. Batton. They're our Ag teachers from school. It looks like they have brought the whole Ag class to help..well, the ones who aren't already here."

Sarah Rose took Fallon by the hand and ran over to the trucks. "Mrs. Batton, this is Fallon Smith. She has horses. I bet you she'd be a good member of your horse judging team at the county fair next year!"

The boys took River and Dylan over to meet Mr. Watts. They went right to work unloading supplies, putting up hay bales, and working together, just like a team.

Mr. Watts walked over to Mr. Welder and Mr. Cowboy and said, "We were looking on the radar this morning and decided to gather up some help for you. It looks like we have a storm coming. I'll tell you, we need the rain, but this storm may be bad. Tell us what needs to be done, and Mrs. Batton and I will get these yard angels to work."

All day long, as the hammering, sawing, sweeping, and yard work went on, the sky continued to get darker and darker. The wind picked up mid afternoon and began to blow something fierce.

When thunder began to roll in the distance, Mr. Smith gathered everyone and said, "We can't thank you enough for all of this work you've done, but I think it's time for you to get on home and take care of your own ranch. Mr. Watts and Mrs. Batton, thank you for bringing all these young people, too. Why, they already have the ground broken to put in Maggie's garden. I just bet River, Dylan, and Fallon will be the first ones signing up for Ag class when we take them to get registered for school. They were really nervous about changing schools, but, thanks to you, I think they have so many new friends that it will help them a lot."

As they said their goodbyes, trucks were loaded up and everyone was waving as they pulled out of the yard. Little did they know how much their lives would change in just a few hours.

The Smith family turned to go into their new house, but Fallon held back. She headed to the barn instead to check on her horses.

She was feeling mighty anxious about this storm. She guessed she'd always feel scared when the skies turned black like they were doing now.

## Chapter Five

The Cowboys made it home just in time for the skies to open up and the rain to start pouring down. Cody and Clint dashed for the barn, laughing together as they ran through mud puddles. Cody couldn't help but think how good the wet earth smelled, even with the smells of the farm mixed in.

Just inside the barn, Otis and Gibbs waited to greet them. Even in the rain, Otis usually ran out to greet the boys, but today he waited in the barn. Cody was kind of glad, too, because nothing smelled good about a big wet bulldog.

Even Ol' Scout was hiding behind the hay bales, waiting for his supper. "Well," Cody thought, "I might not be able to pet that cat, but he's beginning to act like he is staying. Reckon I might as well feed him, too."

The boys went about their barn chores. Clint dipped up feed  and filled water buckets while Cody put out fresh hay. It was a job they had done every day, twice a day, for most of their lives.

When they got to the end of the barn, they both expected the gate to be open and Boloney to be out running around.

The fuzzy black and white pony had a reputation around the ranch. There wasn't a gate he couldn't open or a knot he couldn't untie. That pony loved to cause mischief. Why, one time he got loose at the county fair, and they found him in the cotton candy stand, happily eating and making a mess.

Today, the gate was closed, though. Boloney was standing quietly, waiting to be fed. He didn't raise his head or nicker softly like he usually did at supper time. He was standing by the gate ready to eat, though. The boys gave him a good brushing while they were in his stall.

That old pony was a lot of trouble, but the boys loved him very much.

By the time Cody and Clint had finished their chores, the rain was coming down even harder, and the wind was picking up.

They didn't think the sky could get any darker, but it seemed like it was rolling in darkness with the wind. Off in the distance, lightning cracked, followed by a boom of thunder. That did it!

The boys took off like a shot for the house, with Otis and Gibbs right on their heels. Usually, Gibbs couldn't keep up, but he was tearing across the yard today with his ears blowing back. Another crash of thunder sounded in the distance just as they reached the safety of the porch.

Mama Cowboy came out with towels and said, "Dry off, boys, and get inside. Dry the dogs and let them in the mud room. This storm is making me feel uneasy." The boys did as they were told and got inside quickly.

Ol' Gibbs was so happy to get to come inside that he threw back his head and let out a boo-woo howl.

Daddy Cowboy looked out the kitchen window as the family sat down to supper. Something was different about this storm. Yes sir...it was going to be a bad one.

All through the night the storm built. The wind howled and the rain blew up for what seemed like hours. Every now and then a limb would hit the side of the house.

Daddy Cowboy couldn't rest. He walked from window to window, watching as the storm tore through the ranch. Every time lightning lit up the sky, he'd check on the barn to make sure the animals were safe.

Finally, he wore himself out and lay down to get some rest. He knew that there would be lots of repairs on the fences tomorrow if the storm kept up much longer.

Drifting off to sleep, he said a little prayer over his family, the ranch, and all the neighbors in Stone County.

## Chapter Six

The next morning, Daddy Cowboy sat up with a start at the sound coming from the mudroom. Bam, bam, bam. There it went again.

He knew Otis and Gibbs had stayed in overnight, but he couldn't imagine two dogs making that kind of racket.

He took off to the kitchen and opened the mudroom door. There stood Boloney, looking mighty proud of himself. He was rooting around in Mama Cowboy's mop bucket looking for his breakfast.

Daddy Cowboy knew Boloney could get out of any gate or fence that was ever made, but how in the world did he get in the house?

About that time, Clint slipped his small hand into his daddy's hand. "Daddy, don't whoop me, but I just couldn't leave ol' Boloney out there in that storm. I ain't never seen nothing like all that lightning. When you fell asleep, I got really scared with nobody watching. What if the barn blowed away, Daddy? So, I went out and brought him here with Otis and Gibbs. You ain't mad, are you Daddy?" Clint asked all in one breath.

Daddy Cowboy leaned over and picked up his young son and held him close. Trying not to laugh, all he could say was, "Don't say 'ain't', Clint. And no, I'm not mad. Take Boloney back to the barn, and I'll get Cody. Let's go see how bad that storm was."

Clint got Boloney by the halter and opened the back door to go to the barn. What he saw stopped him in his tracks. It seemed like everything was just broken everywhere he looked. Clint decided to wait on his dad and Cody before he crossed the yard to the barn.

Soon, Daddy Cowboy and Cody joined Clint on the porch. Cody said, "My goodness. I don't even know where to start. Look at this mess!"

Mama Cowboy came out on the porch in time to watch her three men cross the yard to the barn. She looked around her yard. She wanted to cry, but, instead, she decided to be very thankful that they were ok and safe.

With a determined look, she turned and went back into the kitchen. She had flapjacks to make. Her men would need a good breakfast before they went to work.

She reached over to turn on the lights, only to find that the power had been knocked out. Well, there was only one thing to do, she thought, as she went out on the porch to light the grill.

Out at the barn, Clint looked a little unsure of what he should be doing.

Cody walked over to his little brother and put his arm around his shoulder. Cody said, "Look, buddy. I'm a little bit scared, too. But we are Cowboys. We will work hard together, and in no time we'll have this mess picked up. It's how we are. Just remember: as long as we are ok, the ranch will be ok."

Daddy Cowboy couldn't help but smile when he heard his boys talking. They were right, too. All this mess that was broken was just stuff, but they were Cowboys, and they'd be ok.

With that, they started looking through the stalls to make sure all of their horses were ok. They'd see about the cattle later.

## Chapter Seven

Back in Stone County, people were gathering up to talk about the storm. Hank spotted Sara Rose and ran over to check on her. "Man, Sara Rose, that was some storm, wasn't it? Is your shop ok? Where's your mama?" Hank asked excitedly.

Sara Rose said, "We are ok, Hank. What about your place? Seems like everybody in town has a little damage. I was about to go over to the Farmer's Market to see if I could help anywhere. My mom is already over there."

She continued, "You should come help, too. Go ask your mom and then come if you can." With that, Sara Rose made her way over towards the crowd.

When Hank showed up, it seemed like everybody but the Cowboys and the Smiths had made their way to town. Hank was feeling concerned that his friends weren't in town with everybody else.

Suddenly, he ran over to his dad and said, "I have an idea, Dad. I bet the Cowboys need our help. Our truck is still loaded up from helping the new family yesterday," he said.

"Would you ask some of the other men if they could come with us? Our place is ok, so I think we should help our neighbors. What do you think?" he asked.

Mr. Welder was feeling mighty proud right then. Just when had his young son gotten to be so grown up and responsible? He called out to the men standing around. Just like that, everyone was headed home to get their supplies.

Henry and Jessie Brooke Welder met Kate Tucker at the square. About the same time, Mr. Watts and Mrs. Batton pulled up.

Mr. Watts said, "We've been out to just about every place we could reach to check on people. Mrs. Naomi is fine. Her chickens are everywhere, but she is safe." Mrs. Naomi was an older lady who lived by herself on the edge of town. She raised chickens and sold eggs at the Farmer's Market every Saturday.

"We heard about the run-in Mrs. Naomi had with the fox last year. Since she can't afford to lose any more chickens, I sent Mrs. Watts over there with Mae and Sammy. They will have those chickens rounded up in no time," said Mr. Watts.

Mr. and Mrs. Watts raised Welsh Corgi dogs. Not too many people knew about these short dogs until Mr. Watts came to teach in Stone County. It didn't take long for every student to fall in love with these herding dogs.

Mr. Watts knew that since Corgis were taught to herd, starting with ducks, they could round up Mrs. Naomi's chickens and wouldn't hurt or scare them.

Kate smiled at Mr. Watts and said, "I'll go out to Mrs. Naomi's place first to help your wife. I bet by the time I get there, though, the only thing I'll have to do is get Sammy out of Mrs. Naomi's lap." They all laughed at that.

Everyone knew Mae was all business when she "worked," but Sammy did just enough to get finished; then it was time to be held by someone. He didn't even care whose lap it was.

Mrs. Batton looked around the market square, trying to see which Ag students might be missing. "I don't see Cody or Clint Cowboy. It's just not like them to not show up to help," she said. "And what about the family we helped yesterday? Anybody heard from the Smiths?" she asked.

Before she even got an answer, another truck pulled into the square. Out jumped River, Dylan, and Fallon, ready to help just like they had always belonged in Stone County.

Billy and Maggie Smith came up behind them. Even Mrs. Patsy came along. After all, they had just been through a terrible storm. They remembered how so many people had helped them after the hurricane. Now it was time to help someone else.

That left the Cowboys. Something had to be very wrong at the Cowboy Ranch. This wasn't like them.

No, this wasn't like them at all.

Chapter Eight

Back at the Cowboy Ranch, Cody and Clint worked together to get the horses fed. The boys had to push and pull tree limbs out of the way in what seemed like every stall.   So far, all of their horses were ok.

They were both glad that Clint snuck Boloney into the house because the last two stalls on the end of the barn were smashed under a big tree.  Clint knew Boloney was ok, but where was Chrissy?  The best mare on the whole ranch lived in the stall next to Boloney.

The boys ran wide open to the end of the barn. Cody turned to his brother and shouted, "Go get daddy, quick, Clint. Hurry!" Clint took off to look for his Daddy.

When Daddy Cowboy and Clint got back to the barn, Cody was still standing right in the same place. He wanted to look under the tree, but he was scared of what he would find.

Being very careful, Daddy Cowboy eased around the big tree. He looked as far as he could see under and behind it.

"Cody!" he shouted, "Go around behind the barn. It looks like the back of the stall is busted out. I don't see her under the tree! Go see if maybe Chrissy made it out of here."

Cody took off around the barn to look. He stopped dead in his tracks when he saw the chestnut mare standing still between two big tree limbs. She was trapped, but she looked like she was unharmed. Very quietly, so as not to scare her, Cody eased up as close as he could to the mare.

He talked gently to her. "Easy, girl. Be quiet. We can get you out soon. You're a good girl, Chrissy." Most horses would have fought and struggled to find themselves trapped in such a mess, but Chrissy wasn't like most horses. She knew she had to be still and wait for help to come.

Raising his voice a little, but not too much, Cody said, "Daddy, can you hear me? Chrissy is back here. Come back here, but come slow. Daddy, she's ok, I think, but she is trapped something terrible."

Daddy Cowboy turned to Clint and said, "Go get your mama and meet me behind the barn. Be careful, son. And help your mama over all these limbs. Tell her to bring some old towels if she can. We need to get Chrissy dry and keep her calm until we can get her out." For the first time in his young life, Clint walked gently away instead of running full force, like he always did.

This was one time he was going to be 'sponsible, he thought.

## Chapter Nine

Mama Cowboy climbed over to stand by Chrissy and look at her real good to see if she was hurt anywhere. So far, all she saw was a cut on her back leg, but it didn't seem too bad. For nearly an hour, the whole Cowboy family pushed, pulled, cut, and dragged limbs out from around Chrissy, but they couldn't get her out.

Covered in sweat and dirt, Clint brought Chrissy a small bucket of fresh water, knowing she must be just as tired as they were.

Shimmying over and under limbs, he handed the bucket to his mama. The mare drank thirstily and leaned her weight against one of the big limbs to rest. Feeling very worried, Daddy Cowboy looked over to Mama Cowboy and gave her a look as if to say, "I just don't know what to do here."

He knew he couldn't get the tractor close enough to pull the tree, and, if he did, the whole thing could fall on all of them.

Suddenly, Otis threw his head up and turned towards the road. A deep, rumbling growl rose from his chest. Otis took off towards the front of the barn with Gibbs right behind him. What was that sound? That sure didn't sound like ranch sounds. Why, it sounded like chainsaws!! Help was coming!!

Cody said, "You hear that, Daddy? You hear all that noise? Our friends must be ok, and they are coming to help us." Relief washed over the whole family as the sound of chainsaws got closer and closer to the barn.

Cody scooted back out of the tree limbs and grabbed Clint. "Come on. Let's go tell them where we are, Clint." The boys headed out of the barn and towards the sound of the saws.

When they got to the head of the driveway, they just stood there. They couldn't believe what they were seeing. Truck after truck was parked along their fences.

Neighbors were everywhere. Some men were already pulling fence wire, while Dylan and River were helping Layla gather up the cattle that seemed to be all over the place.

Dylan knew Layla would be a big help, but he just didn't know it would be this soon.

Henry Welder and Billy Smith were cutting tree limbs out of the driveway, while their young friends dragged the limbs to the side. Cody ran out to greet them.

He wanted to grab Mr. Welder in a hug, but, being a boy, he stuck his hand out to shake the grown men's hands.

"We are sure glad to see y'all, ain't we, Cody? We got a mess at the barn. Our barn is busted and there are limbs everywhere and our cows are everywhere, too," Clint said.

"My mama and daddy are out back with Chrissy. That big old tree has her trapped real good. Yes, sir. We are so glad to see all of you," Clint continued in his usual, excited way.

Clint ran over to where his friends were. Will Carpenter was talking to two boys whom Clint had never seen before.

Will said, "Clint, this is William and Coleman. Their daddy isn't here 'cause he works for the power company and is out trying to get the power back on. Their daddy has been out in this storm all night, but they wanted to help anyway."

Clint said, "We sure do 'preciate you coming." Clint turned and headed back to the barn. Gibbs came out to meet Clint and walk back with him. It seemed like Gibbs knew just how tired Clint was. Sometimes, dogs just know when you need them.

## Chapter Ten

Together, the neighbors made short work of cutting through the drive and getting to the barn. Now, they had the real work cut out for them. How in the world would they get that tree off the barn without causing any more damage?

Fallon Smith peeked over the top of the fence railing and grabbed her mama's hand. "Mama, we just went through this. I know what to do. I'm going to help Mrs. Cowboy."

Before her mama could respond, Fallon was making her way through the tree limbs to get to the trapped horse. Easing up right beside Chrissy's head, Fallon began to speak in a gentle voice as she rubbed the mare's soft nose. "It's ok, girl. I know you're tired. We have help coming. We will get you out."

On and on, Fallon talked to the mare. Seeing that she was in good hands, Mrs. Cowboy turned to Fallon and asked, "Will you stay with her for a few minutes? I need to get some clean bandages for her leg."

Fallon said, "Yes, mam. I'll be right here." As soon as Mrs. Cowboy made her way over the tree limbs, Fallon looked down at the cut on Chrissy's leg. She knew exactly what to do.

Getting one of the towels that had been brought out, Fallon dipped it in the water bucket. Because she was small, Fallon could squeeze between the limbs and reach the cut. Fallon knew it could be dangerous if Chrissy decided to jump or move away.

Ever so gently, Fallon began to clean and wash the cut. She was thankful that it didn't seem too bad, once she got all the dirt washed away.

By the time Mama Cowboy got back with the bandages, she just handed them over to Fallon. A big smile was on her face when Mama Cowboy said, "Looks like you have done this before. Thank you for your help. I was getting really tired."

Fallon turned her head so Mama Cowboy couldn't see the tears in her eyes. It felt good to be trusted.

Little by little, the group kept cutting away at the tree that had Chrissy trapped. They knew that they didn't want any more of the tree to fall, so they were being very careful.

Cut and drag. Cut and drag. The boys were just about worn out from dragging limbs, when all of a sudden a black and white head popped up right in front of Clint. "Boloney!! How in the world did you get yourself in here?" he asked.

Turning, Clint followed Boloney as he backed his way out of the limbs.

"Daddy! Daddy! Come here. Bring your saws over here! That Boloney has done it again. He's done found his way right to Chrissy. Come look!" Clint exclaimed.

When Daddy Cowboy and Cody made their way around the barn, they began to cut away  the path that Boloney had found.  Daddy Cowboy cut limbs, and Clint and Cody dragged them out while Fallon and Mrs. Cowboy eased the mare through the opening.  Before long, a very dirty bunch of Cowboys and one brave girl led Chrissy into the pasture.

Ol' Boloney took off bucking and twisting, acting mighty proud of himself.

Hugging their new neighbor, Mama Cowboy said, "Fallon, meet Boloney. You'll never meet another pony like him in your life! And thank you for all you did today. You were a big help to us."

After they made sure Chrissy was ok, the group headed for the house. They were hot, tired, and hungry. But most of all, they were thankful.

Chapter Eleven

As they walked across the yard together, they were thankful to see Jessie Brooke Welder standing by a campfire. It was still hot as "blue blazes," but Jessie Brooke was doing what she did best: cooking!

As they were eating, more trucks pulled into the driveway. Mrs. Watts and Kate Tucker got out with Mae and Sammy. The Corgis took off at a run towards Mr. Watts. They were spinning around and prancing, they were so proud of themselves.

Mrs. Watts said, "You should have seen them work! They had Mrs. Naomi's chickens back in that pen in no time."

Kate busted out laughing and said, "And you'll never believe where Sammy was when I got there to see if I could help! Sure enough, Sammy had piled right up in Mrs. Naomi's lap, his short legs hanging off the edge of the swing and looking like he had a big ol' grin on his face."

All day long, neighbors came and worked. It was hard for the Cowboy family to be the ones being helped. For as long as they had been a family, the Cowboys had helped other neighbors. They were really thankful, though.

Besides, that's what made Stone County so special. Everyone came together when someone had trouble.

By dark, fences were mended, cattle were gathered, trees were piled up, and the horses were back in the barn.

Mama Cowboy's garden had been fixed up as good as it could be. There would still be work to do, but the Cowboys just couldn't believe how much their neighbors had done for them.

Everyone gathered around a campfire to rest and roast hotdogs. Off in the distance, Clint saw headlights coming slowly up the driveway. A flashlight was shining this way and that, up high and down low. "Daddy, reckon what that truck is doing?" he asked.

Young Coleman jumped up and said, "That's my daddy!!!! He's coming to fix your power line. You just wait. You'll see. My daddy can fix anything."

All of the younger boys watched as the big truck pulled to a stop. Sure enough, a man got out of the truck, climbed in a big bucket, and started rising up towards the sky. He started to work.

A few minutes later, the boys heard a hum; just like that, the lights came on all around them. The group of boys started cheering and jumping around. Yes sir, this was the best ending to a very hard day.

Epilogue

Long after the neighbors went home, the Cowboys sat on their porch talking about their day. Today, they had learned just how quickly life could change and how important it was to have friends for help. They had been taught their whole lives how to treat others, but now the boys really understood why.

The horses had been checked, the lights turned off in the barn, and Otis and Gibbs had found their places on the porch swing.

It wasn't long before Gibbs was snoring. Across the yard, Cody noticed a shadow walking towards the porch. Stomping across the yard with his tail held high, Ol' Scout walked right up on the porch and jumped up in the rocker beside him. Just like that, the old cat curled up and went to sleep. Cody just looked at the old cat and smiled. Reckon Scout was here to stay.

Sleep sounded mighty fine to the Cowboy family. It had been a very long day. They stood up and went inside their home.

Daddy Cowboy turned off the porch lights and shut the door, bringing an end to a day they would remember for a long time.

Tonight, they were grateful to live in Stone County. Even with work left to do, there was nowhere they'd rather be than right here on The Cowboy Ranch.

72288532R00052

Made in the
USA
Middletown, DE